MERCER MAYER'S
LC +THE CRITTER

OCTOPUS ISLAND

A Golden Book • New York

Western Publishing Company, Inc., Racine, Wisconsin 53404

A Mercer Mayer Ltd./J. R. Sansevere Book

Copyright © 1995 Mercer Mayer Ltd. All rights reserved.
Printed in the U.S.A. No part of this book may be reproduced or copied
in any form without written permission from the publisher.
Critter Kids® is a Registered Trademark of Mercer Mayer.
Magic Days™ is a trademark of Mercer Mayer Ltd.
All other trademarks are the property of Western Publishing Company, Inc.
Library of Congress Catalog Card Number: 94-77864
ISBN: 0-307-16664-3/ISBN: 0-307-66664-6 (lib. bdg.)   MCMXCV

Written by Erica Farber/J. R. Sansevere

LC and the Critter Kids were going on a class trip to a coral reef in the tropics. They were going to go snorkeling and learn all about life under the sea.

The next day Mr. Hogwash and the Critter Kids flew to the tropics. Right before they landed, they passed legendary Octopus Island. The pilot told them the island was guarded by a giant octopus.

Because **OCTOPUSES** are so shy, they live in small caves—if they can't find one, they'll build one! They can stretch themselves like a rubber band to slip through tiny cracks.

When the plane landed at the airport, a taxi was waiting to take Mr. Hogwash and the Critter Kids to their hotel. Gabby noticed that Q-Ball, the guy from the plane, was loading a lot of diving equipment into a van.

The next morning Mr. Hogwash and the Critter Kids met Mr. Hugo and his son, Jocko. Mr. Hugo was going to take Mr. Hogwash scuba diving and Jocko was going to take the Critter Kids snorkeling. Q-Ball was at the dock, too—he was loading a mysterious crate onto a boat.

The **ORCA** is a kind of dolphin. Even though it is known as the "killer whale," it is very friendly, and may be the most intelligent animal on earth.

Mr. Hogwash and Mr. Hugo went to the other side of the coral reef to go scuba diving. Jocko told the Critter Kids that he knew the best place in the whole world to go snorkeling—it was just around the bend.

Jocko and the Critter Kids sailed around the bend and went snorkeling. They all thought the coral reef was the most amazing thing they had ever seen.

After they got back on the boat, the wind began to blow and the water got very rough. Suddenly a bolt of lightning struck the boat!

There are over 300 different kinds of **SHARKS** ranging in size from 6 inches up to 40 feet! Most have never hurt a human. If some sharks stop swimming, they sink.

That night Jocko and the Critter Kids washed up on the shores of a desert island. The next morning when they woke up, LC was nowhere to be found . . .

CRABS have a hard outer shell called the exoskeleton. Tiny crabs may live in other creatures' shells. Their claws are for digging and grabbing. Most crabs walk sideways.

Later that morning Timothy started a fire. Then they all had a meeting to decide what to do.

Pronounced *'conk,'* **CONCH** are sea snails with spiral shells. As the conch grows, its shell grows, too! You can blow into an empty conch shell to make a loud sound.

LC, Gabby, and Tiger explored the island. When they got to the other side, they saw a giant octopus rise right out of the water!

LC, Gabby, and Tiger ran back to the campsite. While they were telling everybody about the giant octopus, Timothy got the radio to work.

Late that night the Critter Kids heard someone scream. They went into the jungle and found Jocko, who had been caught in a trap, hanging from a tree. Meanwhile Dr. Yes and Q-Ball were hard at work in their submersible octopus. They were laying the dynamite to blow up the coral reef so that they could drill for oil.

Small, motorized underwater vehicles called **SUBMERSIBLES** are used for research in cold and deep water. They have greatly increased our knowledge of the underwater world.

On their way back to their campsite, Jocko and the Critter Kids found themselves face-to-face with the giant octopus—and the evil Dr. Yes!

Dr. Yes and Q-Ball tied up Jocko and the Critter Kids. They were about to blow up the coral reef when a coast guard ship appeared in the distance. It was up to LC to swim back to the campsite and light the fire . . . or they were all doomed!

MORAY EELS hide in rocks during the day and come out at night to eat. They let certain shrimp pick leftover food from their teeth and pluck pests from their skin.

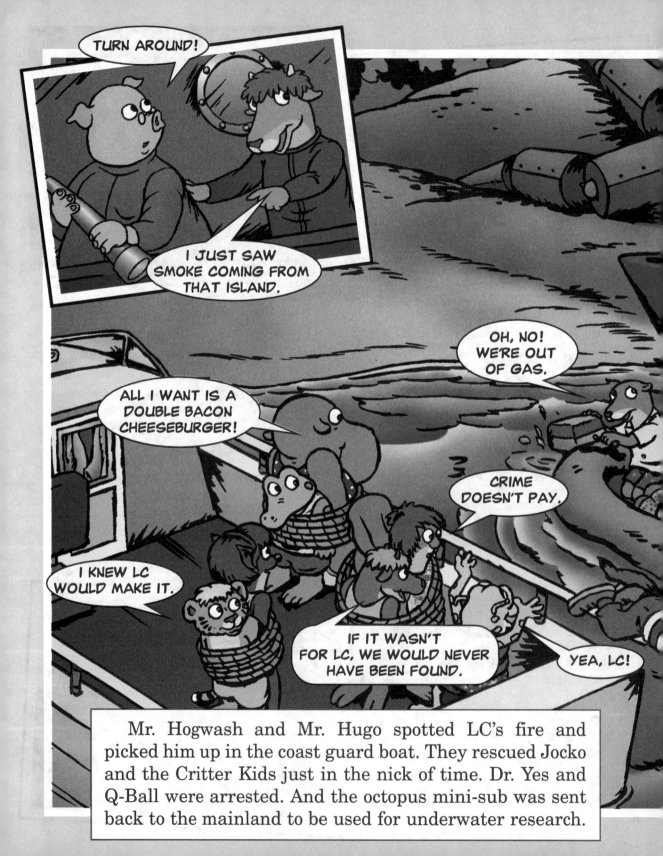

Mr. Hogwash and Mr. Hugo spotted LC's fire and picked him up in the coast guard boat. They rescued Jocko and the Critter Kids just in the nick of time. Dr. Yes and Q-Ball were arrested. And the octopus mini-sub was sent back to the mainland to be used for underwater research.